WOLF LOVER

ASPEN RIDGE PACK: LONERS
BOOK 1

LUNA WILDER

*

This beast just found his beauty, but will he be able to keep her?

Ryder

Life is full of surprises.

For example, I never expected to find my mate, and definitely not in the middle of a snowstorm.

I certainly didn't think I would surprise her and cause her to fall and hurt herself.

Now we're snowed in, and I have three days to figure out how to prove to my curvy little mate that we're fated to be.

Sienna

I was only supposed to be in Alaska for a few days for work.

Now I'm contemplating never leaving.

There's just something about the scarred man that rescued me that keeps drawing me in.

When the snow clears, though, will I choose to stay with my beast or head back home?

If you love paranormal shifter romance books about scarred ex-military alpha heroes, curvy women, or fated mates, then you'll love Wolf Lover! One-click today and see if this Beast can get his Beauty!

ONE

Ryder

WHITE FLIES in front of my eyes and I squint, trying to make out my porch as I carry in the last of the groceries. I'm glad I went when I did since the storm seems to be coming in faster than predicted.

My wolf sighs inside of me, pacing impatiently as I set the groceries down on the counter and start to put everything away.

I know, I know. We'll go for a run as soon as I'm done here, I promise him.

He's been so anxious and bored since we got back to town, and I know it's because we've been staying inside so much. I promised him a run before the storm hit to try to make up for it. I know that we'll probably end up snowed in for at least a few days, and if I don't let him out to stretch his legs before then, he'll be clawing at me, whining to be let out for the next few days.

My fingers reach up, touching the left side of my face as

I think about why I haven't been going out that much these last few months.

The scars there are raised and jagged. I know without looking that they're an angry red color. I've been told they'll fade in time, but that doesn't really make me feel better.

I went from being a pretty good-looking guy to looking like a beast.

My wolf whines, and I force those thoughts aside as I hurry to put the last of the food in the refrigerator.

"Alright, let's go," I tell him as I head toward the front door.

I live in the middle of nowhere. I'm technically still on the Aspen Ridge Pack land, but my house isn't close to the town or other houses at all. That's the way I like it. Even before the scars, I preferred spending time alone instead of with a big crowd.

I step outside, shivering slightly as the wind blows a gust of snow and freezing air my way.

"Are you sure that you want to do this?" I ask my wolf, and he paws at my insides.

I smile. Most shifters just have silent conversations with their animal in their head, but I talk out loud to mine most of the time.

I take a step off the porch toward the tree line, getting ready to shift, and that's when it happens. The wind shifts, blowing the sweetest scent I've ever smelled my way.

What is the smell?

My wolf figures it out first, and my spine snaps straight as he snarls the one word in my head.

Mate!

I can't believe that this is happening now.

I can't help but wonder why now as I race through the

forest, expertly avoiding the brush and low-hanging branches.

I grew up here in Aspen Ridge, and I think I could navigate these woods with my eyes closed. I spent more time exploring the land and terrain than I did at my own house when I was a kid. Even after eight years away, it's still etched into my memory.

I spent the last few years moving around, going wherever the Army told me to go. I was a combat medic, and I loved my job. My wolf loved it too. We've always liked helping people, and I think that I became addicted to the adrenaline rush that came with war. That all came to a halt a few months ago, though, with the explosion.

I was deployed four times, and it was the last one that sent me back to Alaska, to my hometown.

To my pack.

The people are the same, but I feel like I'm not one of them anymore. It's a feeling I've had ever since I got back, and I don't know how to shake it. Maybe it's because all my old friends have found their mate and settled down. Maybe that feeling will go away now that I've found mine too.

I skid around a corner, my wolf snarling and lunging to be let out so that we can get to her faster, but I manage to hold him back. Barely.

A twig snaps just up ahead, and I run faster, my legs working hard to plow through the snow. We rush past a grouping of trees and skid to a halt.

There she is.

She's perfect.

My wolf pauses inside of me as we just take our mate in.

She's about ten feet away, crouched down low as she takes a picture of a fox heading into his burrow. She's so focused on getting the shot that I don't think she realizes I'm here.

She's obviously been at it for a little bit if the snow piling up on her shoulders is any indication, and my wolf snorts inside of me.

"I know, buddy. She needs someone to look after her. Luckily, now she has us."

Our mate tenses at the sound of my voice and then spins around to face me, her blue eyes wide with surprise as they meet mine.

Her hair is a pale blonde, and it's so light that it's hard to make it out with all the snow. She's small, barely even five and a half feet, and I know she'll probably only come up to my chest when I'm holding her.

My wolf licks his lips, and I blink, realizing that we've just been staring at her for the last minute.

"Hey," I say, taking a step toward her, and that's when she stumbles back a step.

I see the edge of the hill before she does and lunge for her, but I'm not quick enough, and she goes tumbling backward.

My wolf roars in my head as we jump over the edge after her.

TWO

Sienna

I IGNORE the cold as I look through my viewfinder at the fox poking his head out of his burrow at me. I can't help but smile as I snap off a few pictures.

My toes and fingers started going numb about fifteen minutes ago, but it will be worth it if I can manage to get this shot.

When I was told I was headed to Alaska to take pictures for Wildlife Magazine, I was thrilled. I've always loved the snow and animals, and any job I can get to combine those is a win in my book.

Unfortunately, my trip just happened to coincide with a blizzard, and now I know that I need to hurry to head back to my hotel room before I freeze to death out here.

I take one last shot as the fox darts back into his burrow, and I'm about to stand when a voice comes from behind me.

"Luckily, now she has us."

The wind carries the rest of what he was saying away,

and I stand, spinning around on frozen legs to see a tall, dark-haired stranger just a few feet behind me.

The man has to be easily over six feet tall, and I wonder how he could have snuck up on me until I remember that I was pretty engrossed with my camera. With the wind and snow coming down, plus all of my winter gear on, I guess it shouldn't be surprising that I didn't hear him approach.

He's staring at me, his green eyes almost looking like they're glowing as we watch each other. He has scars on the left side of his face. They start at his hairline and streak down the side of his face to his chin.

I wonder how he got them.

Maybe I should be scared or worried about being alone with a stranger, but instead, I feel oddly calm. Being around him just feels right, and I frown at the thought.

I usually prefer to be on my own, so it's weird that I don't feel anxious or self-conscious around this man.

"Hey," he says, taking a step toward me, and I wiggle my toes in my boots, trying to regain feeling.

The movement has me taking a step back, and that's all I remember before the world starts to spin and then go dark.

"Don't move," the man orders me as I blink my eyes open.

"What? What happened?" I whisper, trying to brush snowflakes off my face.

"You fell down that snow bank. I'm sorry. I didn't mean to scare you," he apologizes, his face turning red with shame.

"You didn't," I try to reassure him. "Oh my gosh! My camera! Is my gear alright?" I ask as I try to sit up.

"Stay still. I think you really hurt your ankle," he says, concern and worry clear in his eyes.

"Really? I don't feel anything."

"You've been out here for too long. You're practically frozen solid," he grumbles as he prods at my ankle.

"I need to take your boot off to check it out. I don't think you should walk on it, though," he tells me, and I huff out a laugh.

"Well, I kind of need to. I can't stay out here," I point out, and he nods.

Before I can say anything or react, he's scooping me up in his arms like I weigh nothing.

"Put me down! You're going to hurt yourself!" I protest, and he snorts.

"Hurt myself how?"

"By carrying me! I'm not exactly a lightweight," I tell him, my face flaming with embarrassment.

I've always been on the chubbier side, but for the last few months, I've been living off of macaroni and cheese, spaghetti, and Little Debbie Cupcakes, and it definitely shows.

"You're perfect. Light as a feather," he says, then he throws me up in the air slightly.

I gape at him as he easily catches me and cradles me back against his chest. The movement has heat flooding through my body.

Maybe it's some primal thing that makes me want to tear both of our clothes off and climb this guy like a tree. Maybe it's a pheromone thing, and that's why I can't get the image of us naked and wrapped around each other out of my mind. Either way, for the first time in my life, I find myself wanting a man.

I clear my throat, trying to clear my lustful thoughts as I look around the forest. I don't know how he can even tell where we are or where we're going. The snow is coming down hard and fast now, and it's just a blanket of white as far as I can see.

"Are you sure that we're going in the right direction?" I ask him after a few minutes.

"Positive. My cabin is right up there."

I look to where he nodded but still don't see anything. I cling to him tighter as the wind blows back against us, slowing his pace.

"I think I could walk," I tell him, and he shakes his head.

"You can't."

"Are you a doctor?" I sass back, and he nods.

"I was an Army combat medic."

"Oh," I say, deflating slightly.

He smiles to himself slightly.

"Is that how you got the scars?" I blurt out.

I regret the words as soon as I've said them, but I can't take them back. They hang in the air between us for a moment before he clears his throat.

"Yeah."

That's all he says but the way he says it... I just know that it's not a good story.

"I'm sorry," I whisper, and he shrugs, the movement causing me to raise and lower slightly in his arms.

His cabin comes into view, and he picks up his pace, taking the stairs two at a time and kicking the door shut behind us. He carries me over to a comfy-looking couch, depositing me on it gently like I'm made of glass and might break at any moment.

I smile to myself at his care as he sets my camera and bag down on the end table next to me.

"Thank you!" I say, immediately reaching for it.

He nods as he turns and heads over to a fireplace. I

watch as he adds a few logs to the fire, and then he peels off his coat and hat before kneeling at my side.

"I'm Sienna, by the way," I introduce myself.

"Ryder," he says gruffly, and I smile at him.

He blinks, looking like he's in a trance for a moment, and I study him as he shakes himself out of his daze and moves closer to me.

"I really think that it's fine," I say as he tenderly unties my boot and works it off my foot.

He's so gentle with me. He's treating me like I'm made of glass and I've never had anyone act that way with me. I kind of like it.

He pulls my thick sock off, too, and then it's his hands on my bare skin. Electricity seems to spark everywhere he touches me, and it feels like my body is going haywire. Flames lick up my legs, settling between my thighs as he scoots closer to my legs, his hands gentle as they stroke my leg and foot.

A moan slips free from my mouth, and we both freeze. I can feel my face heating, and I'm sure my skin is turning a bright shade of red.

He clears his throat, shifting slightly on his knees as his fingers move to my ankle. I'm about to tell him that I'm fine when I look down and see that my ankle is, in fact, slightly swollen. He presses on my ankle slightly, and I yelp, trying to pull my foot away from him.

"Easy," he murmurs.

"That hurt," I complain, and he winces like I just slapped him.

"Sorry. I...I would never hurt you."

"What?" I ask, confused about why he would word it like that. "I know; I just meant that spot hurt. I must have pulled a muscle or something."

"I don't think that it's broken," he says, ignoring me, and I narrow my eyes. "Probably just sprained, but you should stay off it for a few days."

I turn and look out the front windows at the snow coming down.

"Well, that shouldn't be a problem. I don't think either of us will be going anywhere for a few days."

He nods, and for a moment, I could swear that he almost looks happy that we're stranded together, but that can't be right.

Can it?

THREE

Ryder

MY WOLF HASN'T STOPPED pacing inside me since we knelt next to our mate in the snow to check her ankle. He wants me to bite her, to mark her, and claim her as ours. Then we can ride out the rest of this blizzard wrapped around each other.

An image of my mate straddling me, her curves jiggling as she rides me flashes behind my eyes, and I grit my teeth to try to hold my wolf back.

He growls at me, and I growl back at him.

She's hurt. We need to take care of her before we worry about mating with her, I remind him, and he goes back to impatiently pacing inside of me.

"What?"

I freeze when I realize that I said all of that out loud.

"Do you want some pain medicine or anything? Are you cold?" I ask Sienna.

"I'm really feeling fine," she says. "It barely hurts."

She shifts on the couch, and my wolf and I instantly go on high alert. We're both prepared to pick her up and carry her if she makes the slightest motion to try to leave.

It felt so right to have her in my arms, all of her curves pressing against the hard lines of my body. I only wish she hadn't been wearing so many layers. I hate everything that tries to separate me from my sweet Sienna.

As if she can hear my thoughts, she reaches for the zipper of her parka and starts to shimmy her arms out of the sleeves. I capture the groan in my throat as I watch her breasts jiggle with the movement.

"Fuck," I hiss under my breath.

I'm so bad at this. I've never been great at making small talk, and now after spending the last six months basically alone, it seems my skills are even rustier than usual. I search my brain to try to think of something to say.

I come up empty and curse under my breath again.

I just found her and if I don't get it together, I'm going to lose her before I can make her mine.

"I'll get you some ice for your ankle," I mumble as I head down the hallway and into the kitchen.

My wolf whines inside me, the sound loud in my head. He hates that we don't have our eyes on Sienna, and I agree with him so I hurry to fill a Ziploc back with ice, grab a dish towel, and head back to my mate.

"I'll get a bandage too. We need to stabilize your ankle," I tell her as I set the ice down gently on her ankle. "And we should be elevating it."

I put her ankle back on the pillow on the couch cushion next to her, and she rolls her eyes.

"Did you bandage a lot of sprains in the Army?" She asks, and I shake my head.

"No, I was dealing with... other things," I deflect.

I don't really want to explain that I was dealing with more fatal wounds. I don't need to, though. It's obvious by the look on Sienna's face that she's figured that out.

"You don't like talking about your time in the military," she says, and I shrug.

"There's not much to say. Not anything good anyway."

"I'm sorry," she whispers as I adjust the ice pack.

"It's okay. I'm one of the lucky ones. I'm still alive."

A moment of silence settles over us, and I try to think of something to say to lighten the mood.

"What about you? Where are you from?" I ask her.

I know I'm being a little gruff with her, but I can't seem to help it. Between holding my wolf back and trying to think of something to say I feel like I'm about to combust.

"Texas originally, but I've been traveling quite a bit the last fourteen months."

"Doing what?"

"Working. I'm a photographer, so I've been all over. I just came from New York, actually. I was there for Fashion week."

She doesn't sound thrilled about whatever Fashion week entailed and I file that information away. I nod, encouraging her to go on.

"I prefer nature photography, so I was glad to get this assignment. I love seeing all the animals and I'm really excited to see the wolves you have up here. I've loved wolves since I was a kid but we don't have any of them in Texas. Not outside of zoos anyway. Besides, it's easier to work with nature than a bunch of cranky models," she says with an infectious laugh.

"I bet."

"What about you?" She asks.

"What about me?"

"Where are you from?"

"Aspen Ridge. I was born and raised here. I only left for the Army, and once I was discharged, I came back here."

"Do you like it here?" She asks me curiously.

"It's home."

My wolf paws at me, wanting us to find out more about our mate. Well, actually he wants us to mark her already.

She's human. We can't just bite her without explaining shifters and mates; I remind him.

He growls at me, pawing at my insides, and I sigh. I know he's feeling just as lost with this process as I am.

I don't know how a shifter mating with a human should work. Will she accept me? Will she even believe me when I tell her I'm also a wolf? I'll probably have to shift in front of her to prove it to her.

My wolf howls at that thought, and I wince. I'm going to have to make sure that he's in check before I let him out again.

Will she feel the mating heat or the mating bond between us? What am I going to do if she doesn't? Could I make her fall in love with me before the blizzard is over?

I'm going to have to try. Now that I've found my fated mate, I'm never going to let her go.

FOUR

Sienna

"I NEVER ASKED YESTERDAY. Do you like Texas? Or do you like traveling around more?" Ryder asks me over lunch the next day.

"Texas was fine but ever since my mom passed, it just hasn't really felt like home, you know?"

"I'm sorry," he says quietly and I nod.

"Thanks. It's been a few years now so that pain isn't what it once was."

"But it still hurts," he says and I blink.

"Yeah, it does."

He seems upset with himself for making me sad so I hurry to change the subject.

"I don't mind traveling. I like most of my assignments. I admit that it's getting a little old lately though."

He nods, his attention solely focused on me. I've noticed that he does that a lot. It's like he hates to look away from me, like he thinks that I'll just disappear if he doesn't have eyes on me or isn't three feet away from me at all times.

I've been the center of his attention for the last twenty-four hours and at times, it's been a little annoying, but deep down, I love it. I haven't had anyone really care about me or how I'm doing since my mom passed and I didn't realize how much I missed it.

"Do you not like the food? I can make you something else," Ryder says, already starting to rise from his chair and I bite back a smile.

"It's great! Sorry, I was just daydreaming," I say as I pick up my spoon and dig into the chili that he made us for lunch.

He had already finished cooking by the time that I woke up and found my way downstairs. I didn't realize how tired I was but once my eyes closed last night, I was out until almost eleven this morning.

"Thanks for cooking all of this," I say as I grab one of the grilled cheeses and dig in.

"It was my pleasure."

Strangely, I believe him. He really does seem to love taking care of me. He hasn't let me take a step since I met him. I tried to tell him this morning that my ankle felt a lot better, no pain or anything, but he still insisted on carrying me down the stairs and getting me settled at the kitchen table.

"What about your parents?" I ask him. "Are they still here in Aspen Ridge?"

"No, they passed away a few years ago. Before I went into the Army," he says and I can't help but reach over and lay my hand on his.

"I'm so sorry, Ryder."

"Thanks."

"Is that why you joined the Army?"

"Part of the reason. I wanted to get away from the memories but I also just wanted to see the world. I thought that the Army would be a good way to do that, but it wasn't. Not really anyway."

"Where were you stationed?"

"I was in San Antonio for a bit for basic training. That's where they teach the medics."

"No way! I wonder if we were there at the same time. I lived just outside San Antonio."

"Maybe. The timing would line up."

"Where did you go after that?"

"I was stationed at Fort Jackson in South Carolina but I was deployed pretty often."

"Did you like South Carolina?"

"It was okay. A little too hot for me."

"I'll bet," I say with a laugh as I look out the window at the snow still coming down.

"Do you like the cold?"

"Yeah, but I wonder if it's just a novelty thing for me since it never really snowed or got the chilly in Texas. It's pretty to look at though."

Ryder nods, pushing another grilled cheese my way and I take it with a smile.

I wonder why he's not married with kids already. He sure knows how to treat a girl right and he's easy on the eyes.

Maybe he's like me and he just never met the right person. Maybe it's hard to meet anyone way up here in the middle of nowhere.

I need to get it together. He's just being nice. He's being a good host. I don't want to ruin that by making googly eyes at him while we're snowed in here together.

Get your feelings under control! I warn myself.

It takes me a minute to stop picturing Ryder aiming all of that attention at me in a different, more naked way, but I finally clear away my dirty thoughts and paste a smile to my face.

"What did you want to do after lunch?" I ask and he stares at me with heated eyes that have my system going haywire.

Maybe I'm not the only one having naughty thoughts...

FIVE

Ryder

WHAT DO *I want to do?*

Bite her! My wolf screams inside my head and I have to agree with him.

She's just so perfect. I mean, I knew that my mate would be. Fate doesn't mess up that way, but I wonder if she would be on board with me claiming her. I know that humans usually spend more than twenty-four hours with each other before they decide to spend the rest of their lives together.

If she was a shifter, this would all be so much easier. She would be able to smell that we were meant to be. I need to tread carefully here.

My wolf growls in my head and I roll my eyes. I know that he's furious with me, but deep down, he knows that we need to slow things down with her.

A new scent hits me and my wolf lunges as soon as he recognizes what it is.

Her arousal.

All this time I've been trying to figure out how to get Sienna to fall for me. Never once did I think that she would be attracted to me.

Maybe it is possible though. She's never once shied away from my scars. She barely even seemed to notice them when we first met and her eyes haven't lingered on them once. Being around her has actually made me forget about them.

Sienna might not need as much convincing as I once thought, but I still need to figure out how to tell her about shifters and mates.

"Did you want to watch a movie or something?" She asks and I remember that she asked me what I wanted to do.

"Sure. I'll carry you into the living room and you can pick a movie while I clean up the kitchen."

"I can help clean up. It's the least that I could do after you made us lunch."

"No, you still need to rest your ankle," I tell her and I see her roll her eyes.

I know that I might be coming off as overbearing but I can't seem to stop it. Not when I'm just trying to keep her safe.

"Do you have any siblings in Aspen Ridge?" She asks as I scoop her up in my arms.

"No, I was an only child."

"Me too! Did you ever want a sibling?"

"Not really. I had some friends in town and it was nice to get all of my parents' attention. What about you?" I ask as I set her down on the couch and pull a blanket over her legs.

"Sometimes, but I liked that it was just my mom and me. She worked a lot so sometimes I wished that I had someone to hang out with but it gave me time to focus on photography."

"Have you always liked photography?" I ask as I move to build up the fire in the fireplace.

"Always. My mom bought me my first camera. She was big on recording memories. I had to pose for like fifty pictures whenever I was doing anything special. First day of school was like a photoshoot. We had like a million pictures of me by the time that I graduated from high school," she jokes.

"I bet you were a cute kid," I blurt out and I see her cheeks turn a pretty shade of pink.

She tries to hide her smile but I can still see the corners of her lips tipping up.

"I was alright," she says quietly and I smile.

"I bet you were just as beautiful as you are now."

She looks away from me and I stand to head into the kitchen to clean up and grab her something warm to drink. I've been building up the fires every few hours but it's still a little chilly in the cabin. I don't mind it because I have my wolf, but I'm worried about my mate getting cold.

I mix in the hot chocolate mix and then carry the cup back into the living room. Sienna is curled up on the couch, a blanket wrapped around her as she flips through the TV.

Sienna smiles at me as I join her and pass her the mug of hot chocolate.

"Find anything that you like?" I ask as I take a seat on the couch next to her.

"Yeah, I think that I did," she whispers.

I can see the moment that she realizes what she just said. Her cheeks turn a bright red and she turns to stare at the TV with wide eyes.

My wolf settles inside of me for the first time that we met Sienna. Knowing that she's into us too has him feeling content for the first time in a long while.

I smile as I sink into the couch cushions next to my sexy mate.

SIX

Sienna

I THOUGHT that maybe it was just adrenaline or jet lag that I was feeling these last few days, but I've been sleeping better than I have in a long time, and that weird energy is still there. It's like whenever I see Ryder; I'm being plugged into an electrical outlet. When he touches me, my whole body seems to come alive. I've never felt anything like it before, and I wonder what's happening to me.

I've been trying to test things out all morning. When I brush up against him, the hairs on my arms and the back of my neck stand up. A low dull ache starts forming between my legs when I run my fingers down his arm or back.

I think that I might be driving him insane with all of my touches. He's gotten tenser and tenser since the first time I slid past him in the kitchen. I thought then that it was just because I was walking and he was upset that I wasn't following his orders to stay off my ankle, but now I'm not so sure.

It's become more like he's holding himself back, and I want to know why. I want to know what it feels like when all of that control of his finally snaps.

He's been so gentle with me, so kind, but that's not what I want right now.

"Are you still hungry?" Ryder asks as he stands to carry our dishes from dinner over to the sink.

"No, I'm stuffed," I say as I move to stand too.

"I've got it," he hurries to say, gently pushing me back into my chair.

He pulls his hand back immediately, like touching me burned him or something, and I frown. I don't have much experience with men... okay, I have no experience with men. I'm still a virgin and haven't had so much as a first date before, but I've never seen any guy act the way Ryder does around me.

"You should get some more sleep. I can do up the dishes," he says from the sink.

His back is still to me, and I notice how stiff he seems.

"Are you alright?"

"Yeah, I'm just tired," he says distractedly, and I bite my bottom lip.

I wish that I knew him better. I wish that I could figure him out. He's like a puzzle, one that I would love to solve.

"I can help with the dishes."

"You shouldn't be on your ankle."

"It really is fine," I try to argue, but he spins back to me, and the next thing I know, I'm being swung up into his arms.

"This again?" I ask, pretending that I hate when he carries me around.

The truth is that I love it. I love being so close to him. His carrying me is also the only time I can remember when

I felt small. Dainty, even. He acts like I'm as light as a feather when I'm in his arms, and I can't get enough of that feeling.

He carries me up the stairs and into the guest room. I can't help but notice how he pauses, just slightly, outside his bedroom. I peek in at the master, and my whole being urges me to go in. I want to sleep on the same sheets as him. I want to feel his big, strong body wrapped around me.

He keeps walking, though, and I sigh.

"What is it?" He asks, and I blink up at him.

My fingers itch to brush back some of his thick dark hair, so I gently reach up and do just that. Ryder inhales sharply, and all of my senses go on high alert as I stare into his dark green eyes.

I want to do something, maybe beg him to kiss me, but before I can get a word out, he's depositing me on the mattress and taking a few hurried steps back.

"I'll let you get some rest."

I scramble to sit up, to ask him to say, but he's already striding out of the room. I sigh long and low as I listen to his heavy footsteps head down the stairs.

I climb out of bed and change into one of the t-shirts that he lent me. I had to borrow a toothbrush and brush from him, too, and I take my time going through my nighttime routine before I climb back into bed.

I figured that it would take me a while to fall asleep. My body seems too wired after what happened with Ryder, but as soon as my head hits the pillow, I'm out like a light.

I'm not surprised when the dream starts. I've been daydreaming about Ryder all day, so why wouldn't I dream about him when I went to bed?

The dream starts off innocent enough. We're alone in a field. The snow is gone, and everything is such a vibrant green. The grass and tree leaves blow gently in the breeze, and I lay on my back beside Ryder.

His hand is holding mine, and he brushes his thumb back and forth across the back of my hand. With each pass of his finger, the tension between my legs grows more and more. I can feel how wet I am. My panties are soaked through and sticking to me, but Ryder just keeps up that lazy rhythm.

"Ryder," I plead with him, my body growing antsy with need.

"Easy, mate. I'll take care of you," he says, and when he looks at me, his eyes seem to be glowing with some kind of magic.

I don't care enough to ask him about it. Not when he's finally pushing my legs apart and settling between them.

My clothes are gone, and when I blink, I see that he's naked too. My body warms, threatening to overheat when I take in his naked body. He's so tan and ripped. My eyes scan over his six-pack, my mouth watering at the sight.

I want to touch him, but he moves before I can reach him. He nudges my legs open wider, and I collapse back against the soft grass as his tongue licks up my center.

"Ryder," I moan as my eyes fall closed.

I let myself feel as Ryder's tongue and mouth explore every inch of me. I can feel someone watching me, and I blink my eyes open, my breath stalling in my lungs as I see the giant gray wolf standing next to us.

I should be afraid; I know that I should, but seeing the wolf has me feeling more at peace. I've always loved wolves but never really saw them in Texas. At least not outside of a zoo.

"It's okay," Ryder says, raising his head to look between the wolf and me.

"I know," I say, and he smiles.

He dips his head again, and I bite my lip as he sucks my clit into his mouth. His tongue strokes over that bundle of nerves, and I can't help but scream out his name.

"Ryder!" I cry, my orgasm right there, just out of reach.

I forget about the wolf as I let Ryder take control of my body. Soon, I'm just feeling as his big body pins me to the ground and takes me to a height I've never been.

SEVEN

Ryder

THE MATING MOON IS TOMORROW, and I can feel
the heat starting to bear down on me. My wolf whines,
becoming more restless and agitated the longer we're away
from our mate.

I meant to tell her about shifters and fated mates today;
I really did. The right time just never came.

Instead, I spend more time trying to rein in my wolf and
distract myself from fantasies of bending Sienna over every
available surface in my cabin.

The snow is still coming down hard, so it's not like I
could leave and try to clear my head for a little bit. Instead, I
had to stand there, breathing in her tempting scent, letting
her run her fingers through my hair or down my arm. When
she brushed up against me, I swear I almost lost control and
bit her right then and there.

I need to tell her about my wolf. I need to explain that
she's meant to be mine. Maybe she even already feels it,

which is why she was being so touchy today. Maybe the conversation will go better than I had imagined.

My wolf whines, wanting to go wake her up. We could explain tonight, answer all of her questions, and be buried inside her by morning. Then we can spend all day tomorrow claiming and marking her over and over again.

I bite back a groan, adjusting my aching cock as I think about having Sienna's naked curves pressed up against me. Would she like my kisses? Would she moan when I sink my cock deep inside of her?

My wolf growls, begging me to go find out, but I can't. *She's probably already asleep,* I remind him, and he goes back to pacing. I have a feeling that I'll be staying up all night just to ensure that he doesn't break free and bite her.

It's late now, and the kitchen is spotless. I know I should go to bed, too, but I'm afraid to be that close to her. I'm afraid the mating heat will take over, and I'll mark her before she even wakes up.

I should just sleep down here on the couch.

"Ryder!" Sienna shouts, her voice sounding breathy and low.

Panic takes over, and I'm racing up the stairs before I can think it through. My wolf and I are both on high alert, looking down the hallway for any signs of a threat or anything that could cause our mate distress.

Is she cold?

Did someone get in?

Is she in pain? I knew that I should have insisted on her staying off that ankle...

I burst into her room and come to a quick halt when I see my mate lying in the middle of the bed, her eyes closed, her face flushed, and her hand moving between her legs.

Abort! Get out now! My brain screams.

Don't you dare move! My wolf screams back, and I stay rooted to the spot, watching in a daze as my mate masturbates to her dream about me.

"Oh, Ryder," she says, her voice dreamy, and my body stiffens with need.

"Sienna," I croak out, and her eyes spring open.

Her face turns bright red when she realizes that her hand is still between her legs, and I want to cry when she pulls it away.

I'm taking shallow breaths, trying not to breathe in too much of her desire. The scent is all over this room, making me lightheaded with need. I want to roll around in it. I want to bottle it up. I want to walk into every room of my cabin and smell it.

My wolf howls, loving that idea, and I grit my teeth.

"I'm sorry. You called my name, and I thought something was wrong," I apologize.

I should back out of the room and let her go back to sleep, but I can't seem to force my body to move.

"Are you alright?" I ask. "Any pain?"

"Yeah," she says, sitting up in bed slightly.

The blankets slip down, and I see that she's wearing my clothes. That only seems to turn me on more, and I close my eyes, giving my head a shake.

She's in pain, and you're imagining fucking her? Get it together. We're a better mate than this, I remind my wolf, who hangs his head in shame.

"I can get the ice packs or some medicine. Let me take a look at it and make sure that it's not swelling."

She looks flushed, and I move forward, resting my hand on her forehead.

"My ankle doesn't hurt," she says quietly, and I frown.

"Is it your leg?"

"No, It's... higher," she says, and I gulp.

"Higher?"

"Uh-huh," she says, and I swear I sway on my feet when the scent of her desire becomes stronger.

"I feel hot and achy," she says, pushing down the blankets more. "Right here."

"Fuck," I hiss when my eyes lock on her panties.

They're soaked through with her juices, and my mouth waters at the sight.

Lick her, my wolf urges. *Bury your face between her legs, and let's bathe in her scent.*

My wolf is ready to lunge and mark her, and I grit my teeth, desperate to hold him back.

Not until we talk to her.

Make her cum! He urges.

"Let me take a look," I say, and I barely recognize my voice.

I had wondered if humans could feel the mating heat, too, and I think that I have my answer. My eyes rake down her lush body, taking in her pebbled nipples straining against the soft material of my shirt and the way she keeps licking her lips and pressing her thighs together.

Yeah, she can feel it.

I can't seem to stop picturing claiming her, fucking her hard and rough. I want to feel her under me, her warm body welcoming my thrusts as I take her. I want her to ride me, her curly blonde hair surrounding us as she bounces on my cock, loving every minute of it. Once she's creamed all over my cock, I'll flip her onto her hands and knees and plow into her from behind, gripping her hips as I slam into her.

I want to have her in every position, in every room possible, but I know I'm getting ahead of myself. I still need to tell her about shifters and mates, but right now, I need to get my girl off.

Then we'll talk, I promise myself.

Sienna is wiggling in the bed, begging me to move faster as I crawl onto the mattress and between her spread thighs.

"Yeah, I think I can see the cause," I murmur, and she moans.

"Ryder," she breathes, and something in me snaps.

I lean forward, burying my face in her core and inhaling her sweet scent.

"I'll take the ache away," I promise, and she whines low in her throat.

"I need you."

I nod, reaching for her panties. I was going to slide them off her legs, but I barely have control right now, and as soon as I grab them, I twist, snapping them and dragging the scraps away from her soaked pussy.

"So goddamn beautiful," I whisper, and Sienna lifts her hips.

I can't ignore that invitation and shift forward, burying my face between her legs.

At the first swipe of my tongue, Sienna screams, her hips shooting off the bed, and I reach up, laying a forearm across her hips to keep her in place.

Shifters don't have sex or even get hard until they've found their fated mate, so I've never done this before. I was worried that my mate wouldn't like it, but from the sounds she's making, it seems she does.

I lick up her slit, focusing on that small bundle of nerves that has her thighs locking my head in a vise grip.

My wolf is quiet in my head as we watch the look on our mate's face. Her eyes are half closed, a sexy flush spreading from her hair down to her tits, and I moan. I love seeing her like this.

I reach up, sliding my hand under the shirt that's half ridden up and taking one full breast in my palm, my fingers finding the stiff peak and pinching.

"Oh! Ryder!" She screams, her back arching off the bed slightly. "More!"

I do it again, my tongue greedily licking up her release as she reaches her peak.

Her body is starting to tremble, and I switch to her other breast as my mouth latches onto her clit, and I suck.

That's all it takes, and she's going off like a rocket. She comes all over my face, and I tease her nipple, my mouth staying latched to her pussy as she rides her high.

Seeing her like this is the hottest thing that I've ever seen in my life. I want her naked and spread out for me to lick her pussy every chance I can get.

I lick her through her orgasm, and when she finally relaxes, sinking back into the mattress, I pull my hand out from underneath her shirt and start to crawl up the bed to lay by her side.

I know that I need to tell her now. I won't be able to hold myself or my wolf back now that I've tasted her sweet nectar and made her come.

I settle down on the bed next to her and take a deep breath.

"Sienna?" I ask, and she smiles as she looks over at me.

"Yeah?"

"I need to tell you something."

EIGHT

Sienna

"I NEED TO TELL YOU SOMETHING."

Just like that, my stomach drops, and my post-orgasmic glow fades. I stare at his face. The curtains are open, and it's almost a full moon, so I can make him out quite clearly.

"You're married," I blurt out, and he blinks.

"What? No!"

"Oh," I say, some of the panic starting to recede. "What is it then?"

"I... I'm... Have you heard of shifters?"

"Shifters?" I ask with a frown.

"Yeah, like werewolves or other animals," he says, anxiety clear on his face.

"Um, yeah," I say, wondering where he's going with this.

"Well, I am one."

"You're what?"

"I'm a wolf shifter. And you're my fated mate," he

finishes.

Maybe it's that I'm still turned on, but I can't seem to wrap my head around what's going on.

"I'm a wolf... and a human. I think that maybe I'm messing this all up," he says as he drags his hands through his hair.

My mind goes back to my dream, and I wonder if maybe I'm psychic.

"You're a wolf," I say stoically and he nods.

He's crazy. I'm trapped in a cabin with a crazy man. I just came all over his face, and I'm dying to do it again, but he's batshit crazy.

"Right..."

"It's true!" He insists, and I nod.

"Okay."

"I can prove it," he promises, and my curiosity is piqued when he climbs off the bed and starts to strip out of his clothes.

"What are you doing?"

"If I shift wearing clothes, then they'll just rip, and I'd go through a lot of clothes."

"Shift?" I ask, and he nods.

"That's what we call it. I'm a wolf shifter, and I can switch between wolf form and human form."

"Are there other animals?"

"Yeah, all kinds of them."

"How do I know which are animals and which are shifters?"

"You don't. Not until they shift or if they tell you."

I frown but get distracted when his hands fall to the button of his jeans.

I try to keep my eyes on his face, but it's too much temptation, and they drift south, snagging on his erect cock. Heat courses through my body once more at the sight of his tan skin, and an ache forms between my legs. I press my thighs together, trying to ease it, but it doesn't help.

"Does it hurt?" I ask, forcing my eyes back to his face and trying to remember what's supposed to be happening here.

He's proving that he's a wolf, I remind myself, and take a deep breath as I try to keep my eyes above his naked chest.

I fail almost immediately.

"Yes," he says, his hand wrapping around his cock. "It has since I met you."

My mouth drops open as I watch his bicep flex as he starts to pump his cock slowly, and I gasp as I realize what he thought I was asking.

"I meant shifting! Does shifting hurt?"

My face flames and Ryder lets out a groan as he drops his hand from himself.

"No, shifting doesn't hurt. It did when I was a pup and was still learning how to do it, but now it's just natural."

I nod, staring at him, and he stares back. I'm starting to get used to the feeling I get every time his eyes are on me, and I settle back against the pillow, arching my brow as I wait.

"Whenever you're ready," I say.

He lets out a chuckle, and I can see something on his face and in his eyes. It looks a lot like love, but that can't be right. After all, we only just met.

He takes a step back, and then it starts to happen. His skin starts to change, fur growing as his face shifts, his nose lengthening as his teeth and nails grow. In less than a few seconds, he's gone from the strong man I've grown used to over the last two days to a giant gray wolf.

My breath catches in my throat as I take in the magnificent animal before me, and I slide to the edge of the bed. The wolf walks up and rests his head in my lap, nuzzling me. My fingers sink into his soft fur, and I scratch his ears before I run my hand down his body. The wolf lets out a sigh as he steps in further to me, rubbing up against my legs. I smile as it tickles against my bare skin. I scratch under his chin before he sits back on his haunches.

Ryder's wolf jumps up on the bed, curling up on the bed behind me, and I lay back to look at him. I know that it might seem a little strange to be lying in bed with a wolf, but it feels natural.

I lay my head down on the pillow and watch as Ryder shifts back to human. He's lying naked in bed beside me, and I blush as he tugs the comforter over us, my shirt riding up higher on my thighs. Ryder's fingers brush against my leg, and I bite back a moan as he covers us both up.

"There's more," he says, and I blink.

"More?"

"Shifters have fated mates," he says, eyeing me carefully.

"Okay..."

"And you're mine."

"I'm your mate?"

"Yes."

"How do you know that?"

"I can smell it."

"You can *smell* it?"

"Yes, all shifters can smell their fated mate. It's unlike anything that I've ever experienced in my life."

"What do I smell like to you?"

"Like nature but also something so sweet. It's intoxicating," he says as he shifts closer to me.

His pupils dilate, and I know that he's turned on. Seeing

that heat in his eyes seems to have some kind of effect on me because an answering fire starts to build inside of me.

"What happens now?" I ask him, my voice coming out breathy and low.

"If you agree to be my mate, then I mark and claim you, and you become mine."

"Are you mine too, then?"

"I have been since I met you," he says.

"What does being a mate mean?" I ask him, trying to keep my head clear as lust starts to flow through me.

"It's like being married, but more binding. I'll never love anyone else. I'll never leave or want anyone else, and if you leave me, I'll die."

"You'll die?" I ask in shock.

"Yeah, shifters die without their fated mate."

"Will this thing between us always be so strong?" I ask, and he nods.

"Yeah. It's only really strong right now because it's the mating moon. Once a month, on the full moon, the mating heat will push down on both of us, and we won't be able to keep our hands off each other."

A moan slips free, and I blink, surprised that it came from me. I don't know when I started to shift closer to him or maybe he was moving toward me. My body feels like it's on fire and I know that I'm going to agree to anything to be with Ryder.

That explains why I've never felt this way about anyone else and why after only two days with Ryder, I'm ready to be with him forever. Maybe that was even why I've always had such a fascination with wolves. He was meant to be mine and I was meant to be his.

"Okay," I say, and he blinks.

"Okay."

NINE

Ryder

"I NEED YOU TO BITE ME," Sienna says, her voice low and filled with heat.

Her body is restless, her legs rubbing back and forth together, and I know she's just as horny and turned on as I am.

I roll her onto her back, coming down over her as I let my wolf take more control. I take the edge of my shirt and tug it up and over her head, tossing it to the side, and I get my first look at my naked mate.

I settle between her spread legs, my cock hard and pointing right at her drenched core. I'm not sure that she understands why she wants me to bite her, but my animal is taking over, and I bracket her body with my arms as I lean down and sink my teeth into the space where her neck and shoulder meet.

She lets out a scream, moaning as pleasure starts to course through her, and I take the opportunity to sink my aching cock into her. She screams again as I pop her cherry, and I feel her come again as soon as I'm fully seated inside her.

I barely give her time to adjust before I draw my hips back and slam back into her. I can't seem to control myself. All of my restraint snapped the second I sunk into her.

I fuck my mate hard as I lick my bite mark, sealing the wound. It's sensitive, and she comes every time I brush over it. I've lost track of how many orgasms she's had, but I promise myself that I'll keep track in the future. My wolf howls in my head, pleased that we can give our mate so much pleasure.

She's so wet and tight, wrapped around my dick so perfectly that I can't imagine ever pulling out of her.

The base of my spine starts to tingle, and I know I'm about to come too. I want us to go off together, and I grip one of her thighs, hoisting it higher up on my hip as I rut into her like the animal that I am.

I make sure to hit her clit with every stroke, and I can feel her start to spasm around my pulsing length. I groan when I feel her start to come again. I lean down and brush against my mark as I find my own release, coming deep inside her.

I roll us so I don't crush her, and Sienna braces her hands against my chest, rocking her hips as soon as she gets on top of me.

"I need more," she moans, and I grip her hips, helping her find her rhythm.

"Take whatever you need, mate. It's yours. I'm yours."

She bounces on my cock, throwing her head back until I can feel her silky blonde curls tickling against the top of my thighs. My hands cup her tits, rolling the pebbled nipples between my fingers as she rides me. She moans, her pace increasing, and I smile.

I lean up, taking one of the tips into my mouth and rolling it over my tongue. I bite down gently and am rewarded when she comes on my cock again.

"Ryder, I need you," she pants, and I release her nipple.

"What do you need, mate?"

"Touch the mark," she begs, and I lean forward at once, running my lips over the bite mark.

She goes off again, and her pussy sucks another orgasm from me.

"Don't stop," she pleads, and I roll us again.

It's only the start of the mating moon now, and I grin as I realize we're probably not leaving this bed anytime soon.

Her hands come up, cupping my face. Her fingers brush over the scars there, and for the first time in days, I remember the scars that have kept me in my home for the last few months.

I've been so caught up in my mate that I forgot all about the attack and the scars that have had me so worried these last few months. She doesn't seem to mind them, and I smile, feeling whole for the first time in my life.

I kiss her palm, slowing my pace as I capture her lips next.

"Mine," I growl against her lips, and she nods.

"Yours."

I kiss her, nipping and licking into her mouth until I'm so lost in my mate that my head is empty of everything else.

Her hips rise, and I know that she wants it harder. I pull out, and she whines, looking at me over her shoulder as I flip her onto her stomach and pull her up onto her hands and knees. I sink back inside her pussy, gripping her hips as I pound into her. She moans, throwing her head back, and I look up into the mirror above the dresser, and our eyes meet. She watches me as I mount her and claim her, and I swear it feels like our souls are joining as she orgasms again and then again.

I love how she's just as insatiable for me as I am for her. That has to be a good sign. For the first time since I met her, I'm happy. She won't leave me after this.

Right?

TEN

Sienna

I WAKE WRAPPED up in Ryder, his cock still buried between my legs. My whole body feels well used, and I smile as I remember everything that Ryder and I did together last night.

He shifts under me, his cock twitching inside me, and I moan as I bury my face in his neck.

"Morning, mate," he rumbles in his gravelly morning voice, and I swear the sound goes straight to my clit.

My pussy tightens around his length, and Ryder reacts, rolling me under him and giving me a few lazy thrusts as his mouth finds mine. We make out slowly, our tongues twisting around each other as our bodies join together. Sweat coats our bodies as we continue to rock together, both of us straining to reach our peaks.

My pussy starts to clamp down on his length, and Ryder's pace falters before it picks up, and he thrusts into me harder.

We find our release together, moaning into each other's mouths as I feel him release deep inside of me. He rolls me onto my side, keeping us joined as I stare into his warm, satisfied brown eyes. His dark brown hair is sticking up in some places and flattened on one side. It makes him look more boyish somehow, a little softer, especially with the scars, and my heart melts in my chest as he gives me a lopsided grin.

A cell phone starts to ring, and it takes me a second to realize that it's mine. Ryder lets out a sigh as he rolls over to grab my phone off the bedside table.

"I didn't think I got service out here," I say as I take my phone from him. "It's my job. I need to take this."

He nods, leaning over and kissing me before he stands from the bed.

"I'll get started on breakfast."

I watch him go and bite my lip as I take in his naked ass.

"Hello?" I answer the call, putting it on speakerphone as I climb off the bed and search for some clothes to wear.

I hope to end the call soon so I can get back to having Ryder inside of me.

"Sienna! I'm glad that I caught you," my agent says, and I hum distractedly.

"What's up?" I ask.

"I got you a new assignment! This one is in Africa. Do you think you'll be finished in Aspen Ridge in the next few days? I can get you a ticket to fly out of there and straight to Africa."

"Um," I say, my stomach dropping as I think about leaving Aspen Ridge and my sexy beast.

Do I really want to leave? My career is important to me but now so is Ryder. I can't imagine not seeing him every day, which is crazy because it's only been a few days.

We're meant to be, though. How can I turn down fate?

"Do you need more time in Aspen Ridge?" She asks, and I bite my bottom lip.

A movement catches my eye, and I glance over to see Ryder standing there, a worried look on his face.

"I'm going to have to call you back," I tell my agent, and I lean over to hit the button to end the call before she can reply.

"Ryder."

"Are you leaving me?" He asks, his eyes filled with pain and worry.

"No," I say.

I can't. Not when I'm in love with this scarred man. Not when I can feel it in my soul that we're meant to be.

"No, I'm not leaving," I promise as I walk to stand in front of him.

"You're not?"

"No, I can't leave my mate," I say, wrapping my arms around his neck.

"What about your career?" He asks.

"I can find something else. I can just take pictures around here. I'll figure it out."

"I could go with you. If you want to go to Africa or wherever," he offers, and I smile.

"You would do that?"

"I'd do anything for you. I've spent so long hiding away here because of the scars and looks I would get."

"I like your scars," I interrupt him, and he smiles softly.

"If I had let them keep me locked away here, I may never have met you. I won't ever let them keep me from you or making you happy," he promises.

"Thank you."

"Of course. I love you, Sienna."

He says it so easily, and my heart kicks against my ribs. "You do."

"Yes. I love you more than anything."

"I love you too," I say as tears sting my eyes.

"Good," he says as he leans down and claims my lips with his.

I wrap my arms tighter around him, rubbing my breasts against his hard chest.

"Does that greedy pussy need my cock again?" Ryder asks, his voice low and husky.

I nod frantically as Ryder starts to back me toward the bed.

"You wouldn't believe that I popped that cherry just last night with how drenched and horny you are for it," he says, and I moan at his dirty words.

We push at his clothes until he's naked like me, and then he pushes me back onto the bed and comes down over me. He grips his thick cock in his hand, guiding it to my snug entrance. I scream as he stretches me wide with his cock.

He leans down, his lips wrapping around my stiff nipple. He sucks it into his mouth, and I arch against him, offering him all of me.

His cock pounds into me, and I can already feel my orgasm starting to build as the base of his dick brushes against my clit over and over again.

"That's it, mate. Show me how much you need me."

I sob as his filthy words send me over the edge, and I come hard all over his length. He licks over the bite mark on my shoulder, and I scream as my orgasm reaches a new level.

I feel Ryder find his own release inside me, and my eyelids flutter closed as he gently pulls out of me. I'm boneless, a pile of goo, as he pulls me against his chest and cradles me in his arms.

"I love you, Sienna."

"I love you too, mate," I say with a smile.

I don't know what the future holds for my career, but I know I'll be happy and safe as long as I have Ryder by my side.

ELEVEN

Sienna

RYDER IS SO CUTE. I've never seen him look so content and proud. He keeps tugging me closer against his side and brushing my hair away from my face. It's like he can't keep his hands off me, and I love it. He's so adorable.

Now that the snow has finally stopped and some of the roads have been cleared, he took me into town. We needed some more supplies, but I think that he also just wanted to show me off. He keeps telling everyone who stops to say hi to us that I'm his mate and I'm staying with him at his cabin.

I've noticed that he doesn't really seek anyone out, and I wonder if he has any friends in town. He didn't mention anyone over the last few days, but we also weren't really talking about that kind of stuff.

"Ryder!" Someone calls from behind us, and we turn to see two big men headed our way.

They're both wearing easy grins, and I relax when I see the friendly, curious look in their eyes.

"Hey, Liam, Bo. This is my mate, Sienna," he says, and I light up a bit when he calls me that.

"Nice to meet you," they both say in unison, and I grin.

"You too."

"Liam and Bo are our neighbors. Kind of," Ryder says, and I laugh.

"What do you mean, kind of?"

"We're a few miles from your cabin," Liam explains.

"But we are the nearest house to you, so, neighbors," Bo finishes, and I nod.

"We're glad to see that you both survived the storm," Liam says, and Ryder nods.

"How did your cabin hold up?" Ryder asks them, and I relax into his side as the boys talk.

I keep seeing Bo and Liam looking at me with an almost envious look, and I frown. Ryder told me that no other shifter would come near me once he bit me. They would know not to since I smelled like him now. So why do these two keep looking at me like that?

"Congratulations on finding your mate," Bo says, and I can hear it then.

They don't want me. They want their own mate. They're jealous of what Ryder and I have.

"Thanks," Ryder says, pulling me closer even though I'm already plastered against his side.

"It was nice to meet you both," I say as they turn to leave.

"You too," they say in unison, and I wave slightly as we head in the opposite direction.

"Do a lot of the shifters here not have their fated mate?" I ask Ryder as I look around at the few people milling around town.

"A few do," he says.

"Don't they want to find their mates?"

"I'm sure that they do. More than anything, but our side of Aspen Ridge doesn't get many visitors."

"Our side?" I ask him as we head down the street.

"Yeah, Aspen Ridge is huge, and it's divided into four sections. There's an Alpha, a leader, for each one. Two of them run our half, and the other two run this side. This side is the one with the town and all the tourist attractions, and our side is just the wilderness."

We pass by a hospital and the sign for the ski lodge, and I look around.

"So, their fated mate just hasn't come to Aspen Ridge, then," I say as I think back to Liam and Bo.

"Not yet."

"Why don't they just leave to try to find her?" I ask.

"It can be expensive. You might have to travel for years, and there's still no guarantee that you'll be able to find your fated mate."

"I'm glad you found me," I whisper, and he beams down at me.

"So am I, mate. So am I."

He bundles me into his side, and we head into the market to get some groceries. I can feel the familiar tingle starting in my core, and I know that Ryder must be able to smell my desire, so I'm not surprised when he picks up his pace and starts to throw things into the cart.

"I was hoping that we could go out and explore a bit this afternoon," I say as we move to stand in line.

"Whatever you want," he says, and I smile.

I've been tossing around the idea of maybe starting a new social media account for my pictures up here. There's not much opportunity for art shows in Alaska, but maybe I could compile my photos into a book or something.

I know I don't want to leave Ryder, not for any real length of time anyway, so I'm going to need to figure out a new plan for my business.

Ryder starts to unload the groceries onto the belt, and I study the candy selection. My eyes lock on a package of Ferrero Rocher, and before I can reach for them, Ryder grabs the whole box and dumps them onto the belt.

"You didn't have to do that," I say with a laugh. "I don't need all of them. Maybe just one or two," I say as I rub my stomach.

"You deserve all of them," he says with that stubborn tilt to his lips that lets me know not to argue with him.

I just bite my lip and cuddle up to his side as we finish checking out. He doesn't know it yet, but he's going to get rewarded for that move as soon as we're alone again.

I glance up at him to see him staring down at me with those heated dark green eyes, and I giggle.

Alright, so maybe he does know that he's about to get lucky.

Smart wolf.

TWELVE

Ryder

FIVE YEARS LATER…

"I'LL GET IT, MATE," I tell Sienna as she sits up in bed.

She gives me a sleepy nod before she falls back to the mattress, and I smile as I climb out of bed and head down the hall.

"Dad?" Comes a sleepy voice from the room on my left, and I stop.

"Yeah, Heath?"

"I'm thirsty," my son says, and I smile.

"I'll get you some water after I settle Rose down, okay?"

"Okay," he says, his voice filled with sleep.

I head further down the hall and push the nursery door open. My daughter, Rose, is in her crib, her little face scrunched up as she cries.

"It's okay, love," I coo down at her as I lift her into my arms. "I've got you."

She whimpers, letting out a few more cries as her little eyes blink up at me.

"You want mama?" I ask her, and she lets out a shaky breath.

I carry Rose back to our bedroom and smile when I see Sienna sitting up in bed, waiting for us.

"Hungry again, little one?" She asks Rose as she cradles her in her lap.

"I'll be right back. Do you need anything?" I ask my wife, and she shakes her head.

"Oh! Wait, yeah, can you grab me one of those chocolates from the fridge?" She asks with a cheeky smile.

"Of course, mate."

I head down the stairs, my wolf curled up inside me and dozing, but he goes on high alert when we hear a branch snap outside the back door.

I crouch down low, my wolf and I both scanning for any sign or sound of movement. A shadow passes by the back door, and my wolf bares his teeth as we prowl closer.

Then a knock sounds.

"Ryder? Are you up?" Comes a deep voice, and I let out a breath.

"Bo? Is that you?" I ask as I unlock the back door.

"Hey, man," he says as he walks past me inside.

"What are you doing here?" I ask him.

"I need to borrow some hot chocolate," he says like it's a perfectly normal request to make at two o'clock in the morning.

"Now?"

"My mate is craving it."

I nod, getting it.

Bo and Liam are loners just like me; their place is only a few miles from my cabin. They're probably my closest neighbors, and I guess, my closest friends. They found their mate a few years ago, and she's pregnant now with their second baby. They helped me out a lot with Sienna's pregnancy cravings, so it's only fair that I return the favor.

"I think that we still have a jar left. Come on."

We head into the kitchen, and I rifle through the cabinets until I find the glass jar of hot chocolate powder.

"Thanks, Ryder. You're a lifesaver."

"Anytime. Tell Liam and Rue I said hi."

"Will do," he says as he heads for the back door.

A second later, it's closing behind him, and I lock it before I grab a chocolate for my wife and a glass of water for my son.

Sienna and I got married five years ago. It was right after the blizzard had cleared, and we marched into town to city hall and tied the knot. Shifters don't usually care about marriage, but it was important to Sienna so it was important to me.

We found out that she was pregnant just a few weeks after that, and Heath was born just before Christmas. We had another blizzard when Sienna went into labor with Heath, and it was scary for both of us to go through that so we ended up waiting a little bit before we tried again. Now that we have Rose, I think that Sienna is happy to be done with being pregnant. Both of her pregnancies have been a bit rough for her. I'm just happy that my mate and kids are both healthy and happy.

I head back up the stairs, smiling as I pass by some of Sienna's photographs that we just had framed. She's still taking pictures, though lately, she's been doing shots of exclusively Alaskan nature. It keeps her close to home, and it's what she loves to do. She just had some of her work published into a book, and I couldn't be prouder of my talented girl.

When I head into Heath's room, he's already fast asleep, so I set the water on his nightstand and tuck him in tighter. He's already grown so tall and has started to shift more and more. He loves going out for runs with me, and I can't wait to teach him everything I know about being a good shifter and mate.

I head back into my room, taking a now-sleeping Rose from my wife and passing her the chocolate.

"Thanks," she says, and I nod.

Rose doesn't so much as stir when I lay her back down in her crib, and kiss her head once, letting my wolf breathe in her scent before I head back to bed.

"Well, I think everyone should be settled until morning," I say as I walk back into our bedroom.

I come up short when I see that my mate has ditched her nightgown and is giving me that mischievous smile that I love so much. My wolf smiles inside me, practically licking his lips already.

"Not quite," she purrs, and my cock starts to harden in my pajama pants.

"Do you need me mate?" I ask her, and she nods.

"Just once more tonight," she says, and I grin.

"Just once more," I say as I prowl to her side.

ABOUT THE AUTHOR

CONNECT WITH ME!

If you enjoyed this story, please consider leaving a review on Amazon or any other reader site or blog that you like. Don't forget to recommend it to your other reader friends.

If you want to chat with me, please consider joining my VIP list or connecting with me on one of my Social Media platforms. I love talking with each of my readers. Links below!

Website

Aspen Ridge Pack: Shifter M.D.

Bitten By The Doctor

Bound To The Doctor

Fated To The Doctor

Marked By The Doctor

Aspen Ridge Pack: Loners

The Grizzlies Captive Mate